Just Clowning Around

Two Stories

Steven MacDonald
Illustrated by David McPhail

Green Light Readers
Harcourt, Inc.
Orlando Austin New York San Diego London

1

Clowning Around

Come on, Dad!

Dad, pass the dog!

Dad, pass the ham!

Dad, pass the cats!

See this, Dad?

Look at me, Dad!

Dad looks. And then . . .

Wow, Dad!

2

What Will Dad Do?

Dad is on his bike.

Watch out, Dad!

The bike tips. *Hissssss!*

What did Dad hit?

What will Dad do?

Tap, tap, tap.

Dad sits on his bike. *Hissssss!*

Now what will Dad do?

ACTIVITY

I Can Do This!

The little bear and her dad did many things together. Make a book to show special things you can do with your family and friends.

paper

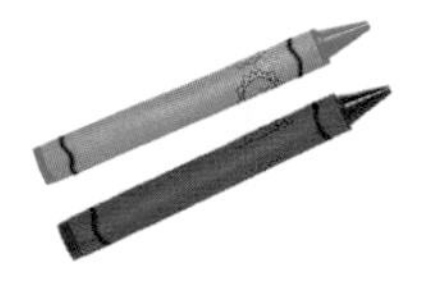

crayons or markers

Fold a big sheet of paper to make an accordion book.

Make a cover.

Draw pictures of things you can do with your family and friends.

Then share your book with your family and friends.

Meet the Illustrator

David McPhail clowns around when he paints pictures. He has fun creating stories about animals, such as the father and child bears in this story.

Many of David McPhail's books have bears in them. He likes to draw bears. They remind him of Teddy, the bear he had as a child. He and Teddy would clown around together.

Who do you clown around with?

David McPhail

www.hmhco.com

First Green Light Readers edition 2000
Green Light Readers is a trademark of Harcourt, Inc., registered in the United States of America and/or other jurisdictions.

The Library of Congress has cataloged an earlier edition as follows:
MacDonald, Steven (Steven K.)
Just clowning around/Steven MacDonald; illustrated by David McPhail.
p. cm.
"Green Light Readers."
Summary: A young bear and her dad, both circus clowns, spend a day showing off their tricks for each other.
[1. Bears—Fiction. 2. Clowns—Fiction. 3. Tricks—Fiction.]
I. McPhail, David M., ill. II. Title.
PZ7.M478425Ju 2000
[E]—dc21 99-6798
ISBN 978-0-15-204816-7
ISBN 978-0-15-204856-3 (pb)

SCP 15 14 13 12
4500620266

Ages 4–6

Grades: K–1

Guided Reading Level: B

Reading Recovery Level: 3

Green Light Readers
For the reader who's ready to GO!

"A must-have for any family with a beginning reader."—*Boston Sunday Herald*

"You can't go wrong with adding several copies of these terrific books to your beginning-to-read collection."—*School Library Journal*

"A winner for the beginner."—*Booklist*

Five Tips to Help Your Child Become a Great Reader

1. Get involved. Reading aloud to and with your child is just as important as encouraging your child to read independently.

2. Be curious. Ask questions about what your child is reading.

3. Make reading fun. Allow your child to pick books on subjects that interest her or him.

4. Words are everywhere—not just in books. Practice reading signs, packages, and cereal boxes with your child.

5. Set a good example. Make sure your child sees YOU reading.

Why Green Light Readers Is the Best Series for Your New Reader

• Created exclusively for beginning readers by some of the biggest and brightest names in children's books

• Reinforces the reading skills your child is learning in school

• Encourages children to read—and finish—books by themselves

• Offers extra enrichment through fun, age-appropriate activities unique to each story

• Incorporates characteristics of the Reading Recovery program used by educators

• Developed with Harcourt School Publishers and credentialed educational consultants